P9-DNV-109

FAMILY REUNION

JANET LORIMER

Janet Lorimer

Fearon
Belmont, California

DOUBLE FASTBACK® MYSTERY Books

The Actress
Brannigan's Folly
Death at the Border
The Devlin Affair
Family Reunion
The Lost Train
The Night Marchers
The Sleepers
Vanished
Voices in the Night

Cover photographer: Michael Jay

ISBN 0–8224–2363–4

Library of Congress Catalog Card Number: 86–81004

Printed in the United States of America

1. 9 8 7 6 5 4 3 2 1

Tori Wayland hurried into the bright, warm kitchen, shutting the back door quickly behind her. Her mother, stirring a pot of hot bubbling stew on the stove, looked up and smiled. "You're late tonight, Tori. I was beginning to worry that you'd gotten caught in the storm."

Tori brushed snow from her coat, and then peeled it off and hung it over the back of a kitchen chair. She shivered, rubbing her hands together. "We were shorthanded at the bookstore today. A few people were out sick, so I stayed to help."

"Sit down and eat your dinner," her mother said. "That should warm you up. By the way, when I got home from work I found this in the mailbox." She reached into her pocket and pulled out a cream-colored envelope.

Tori carefully slit it open and pulled out a single sheet of notepaper. At the top, printed in gold letters, was a name that made her gasp out loud. "Stella Wayland!"

"Your great-aunt?" her mother exclaimed. "Why would she be writing to you after all these years?"

Tori shrugged and began to read the letter. She looked at her mother in astonishment. "You won't believe this, Mom. She wants me to come to a family reunion."

Mrs. Wayland sank into a chair across from her daughter. "A what?"

"A family reunion. She says she just recently learned that she's dying. At the most, she has only a few months to live. She says—" Tori broke off, her lip curling. "I don't believe it!"

"What?" her mother said.

"She says she's been thinking about the way she treated us all these years. She thinks she made a mistake to disown Dad after he married you. Now she wants to meet me and apologize for her cold treatment. She wants to make up for the pain she's caused us."

Mrs. Wayland's eyes filled with tears. "Oh, Tori, how I wish your father were still alive so he could see this letter!"

Tori's mouth twisted into a grim smile. "Yes, it's too bad she waited so long, isn't it. Poor Dad. He was so hurt when she cut him out of her life. She never even wanted to meet you. What a cruel woman she was."

"Tori, don't say that," her mother said. "Maybe she seems cruel, but I've always felt sorry for her. The Waylands are a very wealthy family, but what good has Stella's money been to her? She's a very bitter woman, I think. That's what your father always said. And the other members of the family aren't much better, either. Your father said that when the family was together, they argued all the time."

"Well, that settles it," Tori said, crumpling the letter into a ball. "I'm not going to any reunion. I have nothing to say to Stella Wayland. She can apologize till she's blue in the face. I don't care. I don't need her or her apologies."

"Wait a minute," Mrs. Wayland said. "Don't be so hasty, dear. You may not need Stella, but she does seem to need you. Please try to forgive her, Tori. If you can do that, she'll feel so much better."

Tori gazed at her mother. Then she sighed. "Forgive and forget, is that it? But I can't forget, Mom. Since Dad died, you've had it tough. You've always had to work, sometimes at two jobs, just to make ends meet. When we really needed help, where was Stella?"

"I know it's been rough," her mother said. "I don't like to see you working so hard and trying to go to college at the same time. But that's not the point. Stella Wayland is a bitter, lonely old woman who is dying. If we can make her last few months more comfortable, shouldn't we do that?"

Tori continued to gaze at her mother, a small smile playing over her lips. "Oh, Mom, that's just like you. Okay, I'll think about it."

Later that night, before she went to bed, Tori smoothed out the crumpled paper and read the letter again. Then she picked up a small hand mirror and looked into it. She had always liked to think that she had nothing in common with the rich but cruel Waylands. But that wasn't quite true. There was one thing they all had in common: the color of their eyes.

Tori tilted her head to one side and studied her reflection. She wasn't beautiful, but she was pretty, with neat, even features and short, dark curly hair. But it was her eyes that always drew people's attention. They were a pale golden color that was in sharp contrast to the dark lashes that fringed them.

Tori stared at her face in the mirror and thought about the things her mother had said. At last she nodded slowly. She had decided to accept Stella Wayland's invitation after all.

It was a bitterly cold day when Tori drove north toward the mountains. By the time she reached the entrance to the valley where Stella lived, snow had begun to fall.

On each side of the road, granite cliffs jutted up like the walls of a fortress. Tori shivered, her spirits falling even more when the road curved down into the bowl-shaped valley.

The sides of the valley were thickly wooded with the dark, damp trunks of large oak and pine trees. In the center of the valley was Stella's house, a huge building built of dark stone. It looked like a hungry spider crouching in the middle of a web.

By the time Tori reached the house, the snow was falling thick and fast. She parked near the front, grabbed her suitcase, and ran through the blinding whiteness to the front porch. She rang the bell, then waited, stamping her feet to keep them warm.

The door was opened by a small, plump woman dressed in a plain black dress with a crisp white apron. She had a sour expression. Tori introduced herself through chattering teeth and the woman stood aside for her to enter. As the door shut behind her, the woman said, "I'm Cora Jenson, miss. I'm the housekeeper. The others are in the living room. I'll take your suitcase up to your room."

Cora opened a set of double doors and stood aside. Tori walked on through, and the doors snapped shut behind her.

Tori found herself in a large room with a high-beamed ceiling. There were two giant stone fireplaces, one at each end of the room. The warmth from the roaring fires heated the whole room. The furniture was dark and heavy.

Near one of the fireplaces stood three people, two men and a woman. One of the men came forward with a welcoming smile.

"Welcome to the Black Tower. I'm Neal Wayland."

Tori laughed and introduced herself. Then she said, "The Black Tower?"

Neal grinned. "That's my nickname for this place. Come and meet the others."

He introduced her to Paul Wayland and Selina Wayland. Although Neal, Selina, and Paul were all cousins, they did not look alike. Neal had a thin face with brown, curly hair and a warm smile. He looked as if he were in his early thirties. Paul was a tall man with thinning gray hair and thick, beefy features. Selina could have been any age. She had almost perfect features—and dyed red hair. They all had one thing in common, though: the famous golden eyes.

"Ah, the long-lost cousin," Paul said, grinning and rubbing his hands together. Selina said nothing, just staring coldly at Tori.

"Stella wrote and told us about you," Neal said. "None of us knew you even existed until recently. But I, for one, am certainly glad you're here."

He said it with a sincere smile, and Tori felt that he meant it. She was glad that at least one member of the family was pleased to have her there.

"Speaking of Stella," Tori said, "where is she?"

Neal frowned. "Bad news, I'm afraid. After we got here, we all learned that Stella's health is much worse. She became quite ill a few hours before we arrived. She was taken to the hospital."

"I'm sorry to hear that," Tori said. "Can we go to the hospital to see her?"

"Owen Holt asked that we all stay here. Owen is Stella's lawyer and a friend. He's with her at the hospital now. He promised to call if there were any change in her condition."

At that moment Cora came into the room and announced that dinner was ready.

The dining room was so large that a small army of people could have dined there in comfort. A long, linen-covered table set with expensive china and silver was in the center of the room. Tori took her place next to Neal. Selina and

Paul sat across from them. The seat at the head of the table remained empty, and Tori was reminded of Stella's absence.

Cora began serving a rich soup. As Tori dipped her spoon into her bowl, Paul said, "Well, Tori, why don't you tell us about yourself?" Before she could answer, he continued, "We're all just dying of curiosity, my dear. It's just like Stella to produce another heir to the Wayland fortune. You must feel like a little Cinderella."

He was smiling as he said it, but his smile never reached his eyes. Tori gritted her teeth. Paul had made it quite clear that he, for one, was not happy to have another cousin brought into the family circle.

Tori told them about herself as briefly as possible. She took great pleasure in stressing that she was working her way through college to get a degree in mining engineering. Selina raised one penciled eyebrow.

"Mining engineering?" she drawled. "How . . . er . . . interesting. Not very feminine, but interesting. Cora, this soup is terrible!"

Cora's sour expression grew even more sour. But she removed the bowl in front of Selina without a word. Tori had a feeling that Selina liked baiting the hired help, so she said brightly, "I think the soup is delicious. Cora, may I have a second helping?"

Cora looked pleasantly surprised, Neal looked highly amused, and Selina glared at Tori. She ignored them and said to Paul, "And what do you do for a living?"

Neal laughed. "Gee, Paul, I guess you aren't as famous as you thought." Then to Tori he added, "Meet *Doctor* Paul Wayland, plastic surgeon to the rich and famous. For the right price, he'll bob your nose and remove the bags under your chin! Isn't that right, Selina?"

Selina glared at Neal. "Don't ask me," she sniffed. "I've never had to visit a plastic surgeon!"

"Your time will come, my dear," Paul said cheerfully.

"Oh, shut up!" Selina snapped. Then, to Neal, she said, "Why don't you tell our new relation what you do, cousin."

"Who, me?" Neal laughed. "I hope you aren't going to be disappointed, Tori. Unlike these two, I'm neither rich nor famous. I'm just a poor free-lance photographer trying to make a living with my camera."

"And a portion of the Wayland wealth would be a big help, wouldn't it?" Selina

15

said. "That's why we're *all* here, isn't it? To make sure dear Auntie Stella keeps us in the will."

Tori nearly dropped her spoon. She was so angry, she almost choked on the soup.

Before Neal could answer, they heard the front door chimes ring in the distance. Selina stiffened. "That must be Owen," she said.

They waited in silence until Cora admitted the newcomer. "Mr. Owen Holt," Cora said flatly.

Owen Holt was a small, heavyset man with dark hair and dark-rimmed glasses. Neal introduced Tori. Owen, Tori noticed, took the empty chair at the head of the table. He took off his glasses and rubbed his eyes wearily.

"How's Stella?" Selina asked, leaning forward eagerly.

There was a moment of silence and then Owen said, "I'm afraid I have bad news for you. Stella died an hour ago."

No one spoke as the news began to sink in. Tori felt a pang of sadness and regret that surprised her. She had not looked forward to this reunion. But still, she knew that her main reason for coming had been to heal those old wounds between Stella and herself. Now that would never happen.

Tori stole a quick glance at Neal. She wasn't too surprised to see that he, too, seemed saddened by the news. "He must have liked Stella," Tori thought.

Then the silence was broken by a sharp wail coming from Selina. "Oh, poor Stella," she cried, burying her face in her hands. Her shoulders shook with grief and she began to sob loudly.

"Oh, for heaven's sake, Selina," Paul exclaimed. "You aren't on camera now! No one is impressed by this great performance!"

Selina raised her face and Tori saw that her eyes were dry. Suddenly Tori realized that she'd seen the woman's face before— on one of those afternoon soap opera TV shows. Of course. Selina Wayland was an actress!

"Don't be a beast, Paul," Selina snapped. She took a powder compact from her huge purse and began dabbing at her nose.

"I'm just being honest," Paul said. "Stella was an impossible old witch and she made everyone's life miserable. Why should I pretend to feel sad? There's just one thing I want to know, Owen. How much have we all inherited?"

Tori was utterly shocked at the man's attitude. But was it any worse than Selina's phony grief?

Owen was about to answer when Cora entered the room with the next course, the salad. She was in the process of serving it when there was a loud explosion.

The startled guests cried out in surprise. Selina's compact flew out of her hand, and the loose powder sprayed a fine pink dust over the table. Cora, who had been standing just behind Selina, screamed as the powder flew into her face. She dropped the bowl of salad, and food went in all directions.

"You clumsy idiot!" Selina shrieked, clawing chopped tomatoes from her hair.

But Cora cried on and on in a frenzy of pain. Then she bolted from the room, her hands covering her face.

"Come on," Neal shouted, jumping to his feet. "Let's find out what that explosion was." He ran from the room, followed by Owen and Paul. Paul was swearing as he wiped salad dressing from the front of his expensive suit.

Tori hurried after Cora. The housekeeper had acted as if she were in terrible pain, and Tori was worried about her. She stopped for a moment in the large, gleaming kitchen. Then she saw that the house-keeper's rooms were right off the kitchen. From behind a closed door she heard water running.

"Cora, can I help you?" Tori called through the closed door.

"I—I'm all right, miss," Cora stammered in a shaky voice. "I'm sorry about the mess. I'll come out in a minute and clean it up."

"Don't worry about that," Tori said. "I can clean it up. It's your eyes I'm worried about. Are you badly hurt?"

"No, miss, I'll be all right."

Tori went back to the dining room and began to clean up the spilled salad. Selina didn't bother to move from her chair. While Tori was scrubbing the remains of salad dressing from the carpet, Owen and Neal returned. Neal knelt down and began to help Tori.

"What happened out there?" she asked.

"Snowslide," he said. "At the entrance to the valley. Probably too much snow packed on those cliffs and it broke loose. We think the road is likely blocked."

Tori stared at him in horror. "You mean we're trapped here?"

"For a few hours anyway. Paul's gone to telephone for help. As soon as a work crew can get up here, the road will be cleared. How's Cora?"

"She says she's all right. But she certainly got a lot of that powder in her eyes."

At that moment Paul came into the dining room. His face was gray with fear. "The phone is dead," he said. "The snowslide must have knocked the lines down."

Tori turned to look at Neal. "So we *are* trapped here," she said.

N̲o one had any appetite left after Neal explained that they were cut off entirely. Cora did not come back, and Tori hoped the poor woman had gone to bed. She deserved the rest. Selina complained once about the lack of service and Tori snapped at her. "If you want something, get it yourself!"

Selina glared at Tori but said nothing.

Owen suggested they all go to the library. It was a smaller, cozier room. The walls were lined with bookshelves and the furniture was more casual.

"Paul, you asked about the will," Owen said, opening his briefcase. "I might as well tell you all now and get it over with. The will is quite simple. Stella left a small amount to her favorite charity and—"

"Charity?" Paul said in surprise. "What charity?"

"A home for unwanted children," Owen said. "The people who run the home find families for those children."

"Well, well!" Selina sneered. "Stella had a soft spot in her heart after all!"

"Knock it off, Selina," Neal snapped. Tori saw that he was quite angry, and she realized that he was as disgusted as she was.

"As for the bulk of the estate, it is to be divided equally among Stella's living heirs. That would be the four of you. However, if one of you dies, your portion will then be divided among the rest of the heirs."

Paul cackled with laughter. "Wonderful! We'd all better take very good care of ourselves. Dear Stella. Still trying to turn us against each other."

Suddenly Tori knew that if she didn't get out of that room she would be sick. She stood up abruptly. "Excuse me," she said. "I'm kind of tired. I think I'll go upstairs to my room."

Neal stood up, too. "Good idea," he said between gritted teeth.

When they were out in the hall, Tori took a deep breath. "What a pair of creeps," she exclaimed.

"I know," Neal said as they started up the stairs. "They're the reason I stopped coming to Stella's family gatherings. I haven't been here for nearly two years. I hoped things might have changed, but they haven't."

"How can they act like that?" Tori said. "They don't care a bit that Stella is dead."

"Part of it was Stella's own fault," Neal said. "She did try to turn the family members against each other. It was sort of a game to her."

At the top of the stairs, they saw a figure coming down the short flight of steps that led to the attic on the top floor. Tori was surprised to see that it was Cora. She, too, seemed startled to see them. Tori noticed that she was wearing dark glasses.

"Cora," Tori exclaimed. "I thought you were resting. How are your eyes?"

"A bit sore, miss, but they'll be all right. The light hurts me. That's why I've got these on." She touched the glasses. Tori noticed that the skin that showed around the edges of the glasses was red and puffy.

"You should be resting," Tori said. "If there's work to be done, I'll be glad to help."

Cora seemed shocked. "But you're a Wayland, miss!"

Tori burst out laughing. "Well, this Wayland has spent a lot of summers working as a waitress, Cora. Hard work never bothered me, and cleaning and cooking aren't beneath my dignity, either. So tell me how I can help and then you take a break."

Cora smiled for the first time since Tori had met her. "Why, thank you, Miss Tori. But there's nothing to do now. I was just up in the attic looking for empty boxes so I can pack Miss Stella's things away. But I can finish that tomorrow."

Tori said good night to Cora and Neal, found her room, and got ready for bed. But after tossing and turning for almost an hour, she gave up trying to sleep. She decided to go downstairs to the library to find a book to read.

The library was empty, and Tori supposed that everyone else had gone to bed. She began to search the shelves for a book when she happened to come across several photo albums. Curious, she took the books and curled up on a sofa.

The albums were fascinating. The pictures had been pasted onto the pages in order. Each photo was dated and labeled. There were pictures of Stella's parents on their wedding day. Next came photos of Stella's two older brothers, including Tori's grandfather, Andrew. Then there were pictures of Stella as a baby. While Tori was looking at the photos, Owen Holt came into the library.

"I didn't realize you were still up," he said.

Tori explained that she couldn't sleep. "I found these photo albums," she said. "I never really knew this side of my family, and I'm curious. Can you tell me about Stella's life?"

Owen nodded and sat down beside her. "She didn't have a very happy one," he said. "Her mother died when she was born, and her father raised her. He was very protective of his only daughter. Stella felt quite smothered. She had almost no freedom."

Tori came to a section of photos in which Stella did not appear. "It looks as if she got away for a while," she said.

Owen nodded his head. "Stella's one big mistake! Yes, she did get away. But it almost cost her her inheritance."

"What happened?" Tori asked.

"When she was 19, Stella fell in love with a young man. His name was Jack, and he was handsome and charming. He showered Stella with attention. They eloped, of course, because her father didn't like Jack.

Unfortunately, the marriage fell apart almost immediately."

"Why?" Tori asked.

"Stella found out that Jack had married her only for her money. Of course, when she eloped her father cut her off without a cent. When Jack found out, he left Stella. He just disappeared right out of her life."

"Poor Stella!" Tori gasped. She was beginning to understand why the woman had become such a bitter person. "What happened to her next?"

"She begged her father to let her come home," Owen said. "At first he wouldn't. It was well over a year before he finally changed his mind. But even then he never really forgave her for running away. Stella never left home again. As the years went by, she became more and more bitter and lonely. She never left the valley for any reason, and hardly ever had any visitors."

Tori blinked back sudden tears. All these years she had been angry at Stella without ever trying to understand why the old woman had become so bitter. Now that she knew, Tori felt quite sad.

She said good night to Owen and went up to bed. On the way upstairs she had a strange thought. She had never seen a picture of Stella Wayland before, yet for some odd reason the woman in the pictures looked vaguely familiar.

Breakfast was not very pleasant for Tori. Cora was up and about, serving the meal in the same formal way she had served dinner. But she still wore the dark glasses. Selina was in a rotten mood and complained about everything from the food to the weather. Paul was sarcastic, baiting Selina whenever he could. Neal and Tori ate in silence and left the table as soon as possible.

Out in the hall, Neal asked Tori to go for a walk. "It stopped snowing during the night," he said. "I'd like to go take a look at that blocked road. If it's not too bad, maybe we can figure out a way to clear it and get out of here."

"That sounds like a good idea," Tori said.

When they stepped outside, Tori gasped with delight. The sky was a clear blue and the sun was almost blinding. The snow glittered like diamonds! Tori had to shade her eyes to cut down the glare. When they reached the snowslide, she peered at the granite cliffs, and then gave a low whistle.

"What is it?" Neal asked.

"Look at the face of that cliff," Tori said. "The rock looks as if it were torn away. Granite is a hard rock, and a simple snowslide wouldn't do that. Unless I'm badly mistaken, that rock was ripped out by some kind of explosive."

"Like dynamite?" Neal asked. Tori nodded. "That would mean that the snowslide wasn't an accident," Neal said. "Somebody caused it to happen."

"That's right," Tori agreed. "Which makes me wonder about those phone lines."

"You think they were cut," Neal said grimly. "Let's find out."

They left the road and entered the thick woods. It was hard work plowing through the snow. By the time they'd traced the phone lines, Tori's muscles ached.

"Well, you were right," Neal said, studying the neatly clipped lines. "But who did it and why?"

Tori shook her head. "I can't imagine. Of course, I can't think of anyone outside the valley who would want to trap us here."

"It just doesn't make sense," Neal said.

Suddenly their discussion was interrupted by a series of sharp screams. "That came from the direction of the house," Neal said. "Come on!"

When they broke out of the trees, they saw a group of people gathered around someone lying on the ground.

"What happened?" Neal called as they approached.

"It's Paul," Owen said, stepping aside so Neal and Tori could see. "Selina found him here."

Neal knelt down by Paul's still body and felt for a pulse. "He's still alive," Neal said. Paul groaned.

"He must have slipped and fallen on a patch of ice," Owen said.

"Perhaps," Tori said. She leaned over and pulled gently at the stocking cap Paul was wearing. Under the cap was a nasty lump.

"Let's get him into the house," Neal said. While Neal and Owen carried Paul to the house, Tori glanced at the other two women. Selina was pale and obviously upset. Standing next to her was Cora. The housekeeper was shaking from her head to her toes.

Neal and Owen carried Paul up to his room. Tori followed them, and then asked Owen to bring her warm water and a warm clean cloth. When he returned, she began to wash the wound.

"I'll need an ice pack to get the swelling down," she told Owen. When he left, she said to Neal, "I don't think he's badly hurt. It just looks nasty. The skin is cut a little, but the cap saved him from a worse injury. The one thing I'm worried about is concussion."

Paul groaned again. Neal said, "Paul, can you tell us what happened?"

"Don't know," Paul said thickly. "I went outside to get some firewood. Then something hit me."

Neal and Tori looked at each other. "We need to talk," Neal muttered.

"Well, there's not much more I can do," Tori said. "He needs rest. Let's go down to the library."

When they reached the library, Neal closed the doors. "We just got our answer," he said in a low voice. "Now I know why the phone lines were cut and the road was blocked. The trouble is, I *don't* like the answer."

"Well, what is it?" Tori exclaimed.

"Remember what Owen said about the will? All four of us equally inherit the estate. But if one of us dies, his or her portion is divided among the others."

Tori gasped. "Are you saying that someone tried to kill Paul for his share of the money?"

Neal nodded. "Someone wants to keep us here long enough to kill three of us."

They gazed at each other in worried silence. Then Tori said, "You and I were together when Paul was attacked. That would make Selina the obvious suspect."

Neal nodded. "I was thinking the same thing."

"But it doesn't make sense," Tori said. "It would be very careless of her to try to kill Paul in broad daylight so close to the house. I know she seems thoughtless, but I don't think she'd be that stupid."

"Maybe she acted without thinking," Neal said. "Maybe she just grabbed her chance and hoped it would look like an accident."

"Maybe," Tori said. But she had a funny feeling that there was something they were overlooking.

"The point is," Neal continued, "that our lives are in danger, too. We'll have to be very careful and—"

The rest of his words were drowned out by a shrill scream and a series of thudding sounds. Neal and Tori raced to the library door and flung it open. At the foot of the broad staircase lay Selina.

They rushed to her side. When they reached her, Selina was already moaning and moving about.

"Nothing seems to be broken," Neal said. "But she has a lot of cuts and bruises." Tori looked down and realized that Selina's large purse had come open. The contents were scattered on the stairs and all over the floor.

"What happened, Selina?" Neal said, helping her to sit up.

"I was pushed!" Selina wailed. "I was at the top of the stairs, just starting to come down, when someone shoved me! I lost my balance and fell."

"You didn't see who shoved you?" Neal asked.

"Of course not!" Selina snapped. "I was too busy trying to protect my face!"

"That figures," Tori thought. She glanced at Neal and wondered if he were thinking what she was thinking. Could Paul have come up behind Selina and pushed her? He was supposed to be in his room, suffering from a nasty head wound. Had he been faking the pain?

Or had Selina herself faked the fall? She was, after all, an actress. Could she be faking in order to make everyone believe that she, too, was just an innocent victim? The trouble was, Tori thought, they were running out of suspects.

"We'd better get Selina up to her room," Neal said, gently lifting the redhead.

"I'll get this stuff picked up," Tori said, pointing at the contents of Selina's purse.

She began putting tubes of lipstick, boxes of eyeshadow, and eyeliner pencils back into the purse. Suddenly her hand stopped in midair over a small plastic case. She picked it up and examined it. It was a contact lens case. Tori couldn't help grinning. So, the perfect beauty wasn't quite so perfect, after all! She opened the case and found it empty. Tori's grin changed to a frown. If Selina had been wearing the lenses when she fell, she might have injured her eyes. Tori decided to check Selina carefully.

When she got upstairs, Neal was coming out of Selina's room, his face red with anger.

"What's wrong?" Tori asked.

"She can't be too badly hurt," he snapped. "Her temper is still the same. She's *demanding* extra pillows and a cup of tea."

Tori grinned slightly. "Maybe that's a good sign," she said. "I, for one, don't like the idea of playing nursemaid to her for very long. See if you can find Cora, Neal. I'll go apply first aid to her highness!"

Selina was lying on her bed looking sullen. Tori set the purse down on the nightstand. "If you are wearing contact lenses," she said, "I think you should take them out. Your left eye is going to be a lovely shade of purple in a few hours."

Selina gasped and grabbed for her hand mirror.

"Oh, my face is ruined!" she wailed.

"Oh, you'll survive," Tori said coldly. "Black eyes are only temporary. But about those lenses—"

"I don't know what you're talking about," Selina snapped. "I certainly have no need for contact lenses!"

"Are you sure?" Tori asked. "I found this among your things downstairs." She held out the plastic case.

"That's not mine," Selina said. "I never saw it before."

Tori frowned. She didn't think Selina was lying. But if the plastic case didn't belong to her, whose was it? Tori stuffed the case into her pocket and said nothing more. But she didn't stop thinking about it.

Neal brought Selina a cup of tea just as Tori finished bandaging her wounds. Selina took one taste and made a face. "That stupid housekeeper can't even make a decent cup of tea!" she whined.

"I made it," Neal snapped. "So don't blame Cora!" Then he and Tori left Selina to moan by herself.

"Where is Cora?" Tori said when they were in the hall.

Neal shrugged. "I don't know," he said. "Taking a break, I hope. She deserves it. Paul and Selina haven't been exactly kind."

"So I noticed," Tori said. "What now?"

"I'm going to see if I can find Owen," Neal said. "I think I ought to tell him what we discovered this morning. What about you?"

Tori shrugged. "I guess I'd better go check my other patient," she said. "I'm beginning to feel like Florence Nightingale."

Neal grinned. "Okay. But remember, be careful!"

As Tori started down the hall toward Paul's room, she saw Cora coming down from the attic again. The housekeeper stiffened nervously when she saw Tori.

"Still looking for boxes?" Tori asked cheerfully.

Cora nodded, licking lips that had gone dry. "Yes, miss, but I have to stop to get lunch," she said. "Do you know if Mr. Paul will want anything to eat?"

"I'm not sure," Tori said. "But I was just going to check on him. I'll ask."

She started down the hall, and then paused. Cora didn't ask about Selina. Maybe she didn't know the woman had been hurt. That meant she'd been in the attic for a long time. Surely it didn't take that much time just to find some empty boxes. Unless . . .

Tori turned around. Cora had disappeared downstairs. The hall was empty. Tori wondered why the housekeeper had seemed so nervous. Was there another reason she'd been in the attic, something she didn't want anyone to know about?

Tori headed for the attic. She was suddenly very curious about it. She saw that the lock was old-fashioned and very rusty. But someone had oiled it recently and the oil came off on Tori's fingers when she touched it. She wondered if the housekeeper had locked it again, but she hadn't. The door opened quite easily.

The attic was a long room with a low ceiling. Small windows allowed some light in, but the windows were filthy with dust and cobwebs. Tori found a light switch near the door and turned it on. The room filled with a weak light from a dim bulb in the ceiling.

Tori could tell that no one had entered the attic until recently. It was filled with broken furniture, boxes, and trunks. Everything was covered with a thick blanket of dust. There were footprints in the dust on the floor and it looked as if the same pair of shoes had made them all.

Nearest to the door, the boxes and trunks had been opened and their contents scattered carelessly about. It certainly looked as if Cora had been busy searching for something. But what?

Why would the housekeeper only now come up here? Was it possible that she hadn't been able to get in while Stella was here? But what would Stella have locked away in the attic? There was nothing of value that Tori could see. If Cora wanted to steal something, why not go after the silverware? Or even Stella's jewelry? The only things in the attic were things from the past.

And then Tori had a wild thought. Little things she'd seen and heard in the last 24 hours came back to her. The picture that looked so familiar. The terms of Stella's will. Cora's nervousness. It all added up to one crazy idea. And yet, if Tori were right, it would explain everything.

Cora had made one mistake in her search. When things get shoved into attics, the older things usually keep getting moved to the back. Cora had begun her search too close to the door. Tori picked her way across the room until she got to the back.

There were a stack of magazines from the 1940s and the moth-eaten jacket of a World War II uniform. There was also a woman's hat covered with faded pink roses and a dusty, torn black face net.

Tori began to dig through the trunks and boxes in this section of the attic. At the bottom of one of the trunks, she finally found what she was looking for. With shaking fingers, she drew out papers from an old yellow envelope and quickly scanned them. Even though the crazy idea had made sense, Tori could hardly believe she'd found the proof to back it up. She drew in a deep breath. The puzzle was complete.

Then she glanced at her watch. She hadn't realized how late it had gotten. Everyone would be wondering what had happened to her. She scrambled to her feet and shoved the papers into her pocket. Then she hurried downstairs.

The guests were already in the middle of lunch. Even Paul and Selina were at the table. Neal was picking at his food, a worried expression on his face. Tori had a feeling that she was the reason for his concern. Owen was again sitting at the head of the table, and Cora hovered nearby.

For a moment Tori hesitated to go into that room. One of those people had already tried twice to commit murder. She knew she would have to be very careful.

"Tori!" Neal exclaimed when she entered the room. "I was worried about you. Where have you been?"

"Crawling around in the attic, from the looks of her," Paul said sourly. Tori realized she was covered with dust and cobwebs. It was a dead giveaway. She heard Cora gasp, but she refused to look at the woman.

"Probably hiding from you," Selina snapped. "After all, she wouldn't want to be the next victim!"

"Are you accusing me again?" Paul said angrily. Tori realized they must have been arguing before she entered the room.

"Well, who else could have pushed me down the stairs?" Selina exclaimed.

"What about *her?*" Paul said, looking at Tori. "We don't know much about our new cousin, do we? Except that she's pretty poor and could use the money."

"Don't be a fool, Paul," Neal exclaimed. "Tori was with me when each of you was attacked."

"Maybe they're in it together," Selina said.

"Stop it!" Tori cried. "Neal and I didn't try to kill anyone. But I know who did!" She realized, too late, that she had gone too far.

"Maybe you'd better explain yourself," Owen said quietly.

"All right," Tori said in a shaky voice. "We all assumed that the would-be killer had to be one of the four of us because we are the heirs. But I believe that there is another heir."

Everyone gasped. "Just who is this person?" Paul demanded. "And what gave you such a crazy idea, anyway?"

"Last night Owen told me about Stella's life," Tori said. "I saw her pictures in the photo album. I thought she looked familiar, although I'd never seen her picture before. Also, something about Stella's life bothered me. After she eloped and her marriage fell apart, her father wouldn't let her come home for more than a year. That seemed strange, considering how much he cared for her. Then today I suddenly wondered if maybe the reason he wouldn't let her come home was that she was going to have a child."

"That's ridiculous!" Selina snapped. "Just a fairy tale!"

"Wait!" said Neal. "It makes sense. Go on, Tori!"

"In her will," Tori continued, "Stella left some money to a home for unwanted children. We were all surprised, I think, because Stella was not the kind to leave money to charity. But I think that years ago that home helped Stella find a family for her child."

"But why wouldn't her father let her keep the child?" Neal asked.

"I think the child would have been a constant reminder of Stella's betraying her father," Tori said. "So he made her choose between keeping the child or coming home to him and being his heir. It must have been a terrible decision for Stella. But she was so young and probably very scared. She didn't know how to survive on her own without the Wayland money. So she gave up the child."

"You still haven't given us any proof," Owen said.

"This morning I found it," Tori said, drawing the papers from her pocket. "Here is a copy of the birth certificate and a copy of the adoption papers that Stella had to sign."

"Where is the child?" Paul demanded.

"The child is now an adult," Tori said. "She's here, in this room. It's Cora Jenson."

Cora gave a loud wail and backed up against the wall. Neal walked over to her. "Is it true?" he asked softly.

Slowly Cora removed her glasses from her face. Everyone gasped. Cora's eyes were golden.

Selina groaned. "It's true, then! We are related to this horrible, dumpy little creature."

"She tried to kill us," Paul roared. He would have lunged at Cora if Neal hadn't blocked his way.

"How did you guess, Tori?" Owen said.

"There were a few clues," Tori said. "The powder that flew into Cora's eyes seemed to do a great deal of damage, much more than you'd expect. Cora said her eyes hurt so much she had to wear dark glasses. I thought there was something strange about that. Then today, after Selina was attacked, I found a contact lens case among her things. But Selina said it wasn't hers. I couldn't imagine who else here would wear contact lenses.

"Then I remembered Cora's dark glasses. It suddenly occurred to me that Cora might be using them for a different reason. If she were a Wayland, the color of her eyes would give her away. I knew, of course, that contact lenses are sometimes used to *change the color of the eyes*. The powder scratched her eyes so badly she couldn't wear the lenses. That's why Cora had to use dark glasses."

"You said something about Stella's picture looking familiar," Neal said.

"Yes, and finally today I realized why! If you look at Cora, you see a strong likeness to Stella when she was young," Tori said. "Also, Cora spent a lot of time last night and today in the attic. I decided she was searching for something. There's so much junk up there, it couldn't have been anything valuable, like silver or jewelry. Then I realized it might be the proof she needed to make her claim as an heir."

"But she did try to kill us!" Paul exclaimed. "She'll never get away with that!"

"You can't blame Cora completely," Tori said. "You see, she had a lot of help. Didn't she, Owen?"

Suddenly Owen stood up. He was holding a gun. "Very clever, young woman," he said coldly. "Just how did you figure that out?"

Tori sighed. "I was almost certain Cora had to have some help in this," she said. "I figured Stella confided in you when she made out her will. And you saw a way to cut yourself in on the estate. So you did some searching and found Cora. You told her about her real mother, and you convinced her that there was a way to get even with Stella. You got her a job here, so both of you could search for the proof you needed to claim her as an heir. In return she agreed to split the inheritance with you.

"Selina and Paul always treated Cora very rudely when they came to visit. Soon Cora grew to hate all the Waylands. It probably wasn't hard for you to convince her that killing the four of us would be even better. Cora would inherit more money that way."

"Go on," Owen said in a soft but deadly tone.

"You set up the dynamite that caused the explosion to block the road," Tori said. "You cut the phone lines. You planned to kill all of us, with Cora's help, during this reunion. Then Cora would be the only heir. The only trouble was that Cora found she couldn't kill anyone. She tried, but she couldn't do the job right. First she failed with Paul, and then with Selina."

"Thanks to you and Neal," Owen said bitterly. "The two of you were so kind to her that she began to realize that some of the Waylands were good after all. However, my plan is still going to work. There's going to be a terrible accident, probably a fire. The house is going to burn down with the four of you trapped inside. Only Cora and I will survive. Come here, Cora!"

The frightened little woman scurried to his side. Tori felt a surge of pity for her. After all, she was also a victim! Cora had been abandoned by her mother, mistreated by Selina and Paul, and now manipulated by Owen.

"Go find a piece of firewood," Owen ordered. "Something nice and heavy. We'll knock them out and then set this place on fire."

"Cora, don't!" Tori begged. "Once he gets his hands on the money, he'll have to kill you, too!"

"Shut up!" Owen snapped. Cora hurried from the room. When she returned, she was holding a thick piece of oak wood.

"Now," said Owen, "the four of you will turn around."

Suddenly Cora raised the club and brought it down on Owen's head. He groaned and slumped to the floor, the gun dropping from his hand. Neal picked it up while Paul examined Owen.

"He's out cold," Paul said, "but he's alive."

Tori put her arms around Cora who had dropped the wood and was crying. "You saved our lives," Tori said.

"I know that you did the wrong thing when you tried to kill Paul and Selina, Cora," Neal said. "But you did stop Owen from killing us and that certainly has to count for something. I'll do anything I can to help you."

"So will I," Tori said. "There was a time when I, too, hated Stella. Now I just feel pity and sadness. Money meant everything to her. But it never brought her the one thing she wanted most—happiness. Maybe with our help, you can find that, Cora."